For Thomas,
Timothy & Mary

Published in the United States
by Xist Publishing
www.xistpublishing.com
24200 Southwest Freeway
Suite 402- 290
Rosenberg, TX 77471

Hardcover ISBN: 978-1-5324-1590-6
Paperback ISBN: 978-1-5324-1589-0
eISBN: 978-1-5324-1588-3

Printed in the USA

Pat a Cake Who

written by
J.T.S. Halvorsen

illustrated by
Alice Pieroni

Pat a cake, pat a cake, Baker's Man.
Bake me a cake as fast as you can.
Roll it, pat it, mark it with a B,
and throw it in the oven for baby and me.

Pat a cake, pat a cake, Farmer Jane.
Bake me a cake in the pouring rain.
Roll it, pat it,
Scratch it with your rake,
and throw it in the oven
for a good long bake!

Pat a cake, pat a cake, Puppy Dog.
Bake me a cake in a hollow log.

Roll it,
pat it,
sniff it with
your nose,
and bury it next to
the garden hose.

Pat a cake, pat a cake, Kitty Cat.
Bake me a cake
that tastes like a rat.
Roll it, pat it,
rub it with your cheek,
give it to a mouse
and make her squeak.

Pat a cake,
pat a cake,
baby chick.
Bake me a cake
on a fiery brick.

Roll it, pat it,
peck it with your beak,
Sprinkle it with worms
and roll it in the creek.

Pat a cake, pat a cake, Choo-Choo Train.
Bake me a cake on the open plain.
Roll it, pat it, plop it on the track,
and bake it in the sun till we all come back.

Pat a cake, pat a cake, Dinosaur.
Bake me a cake with a awesome roar.
Roll it, pat it, put it on a limb,
and share it with the kids on the jungle gym.

Pat a cake, pat a cake, Wildebeest.
Bake me a cake for a great big feast.
Roll it, pat it, stamp it with your hoof,
Stab it with your horns,
and fling it on the roof.

Pat a cake, pat a cake, Polar Bear.
Bake me a cake in the arctic air,
Roll it, pat it, grab it with your claws,
and throw it in the air for Santa Claus.

Pat a cake, pat a cake, Killer Whale.
Bake me a cake
with your great big tail,

Roll it,
pat it,
poke it with your snout,

and throw it
on the beach
with a great
white spout.

Pat a cake, pat a cake, Baby Doll.
Bake me a cake in the shape of a ball.
Roll it, pat it, bake it just right,
save a piece for me as I say good night.